Quick! Quick!

Written by Roderick Hunt
Illustrated by Nick Schon,
based on the original characters
created by Roderick Hunt and Alex Brychta

OXFORD
UNIVERSITY PRESS

Read these words

quick **ou**t

ouch stu**ck**

sti**ck** ja**ck**

The ball shot off.

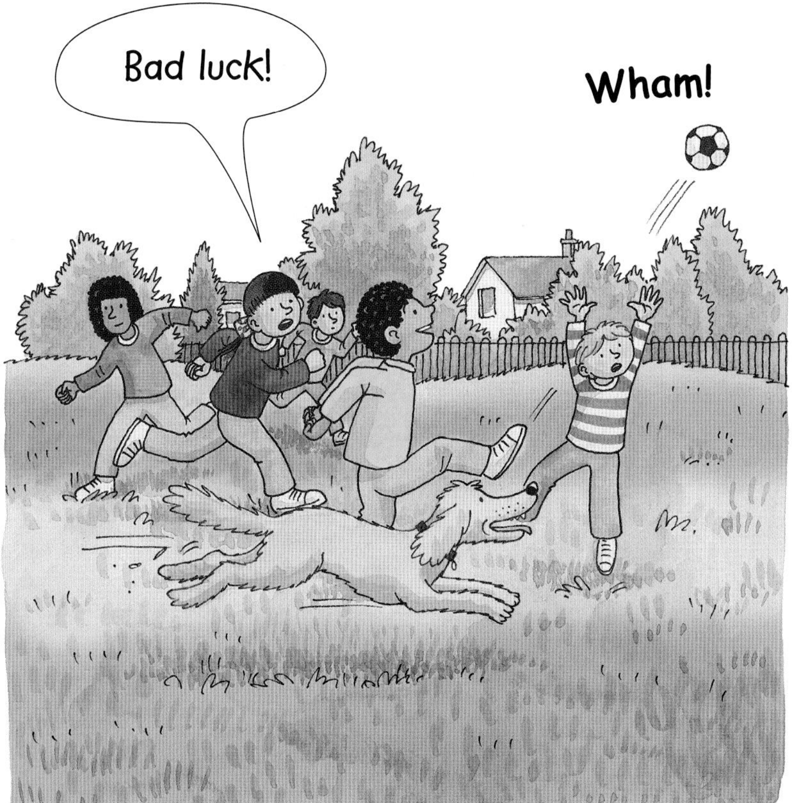
Bad luck!
Wham!

"I can get it," said Kipper.

But Kipper got stuck.

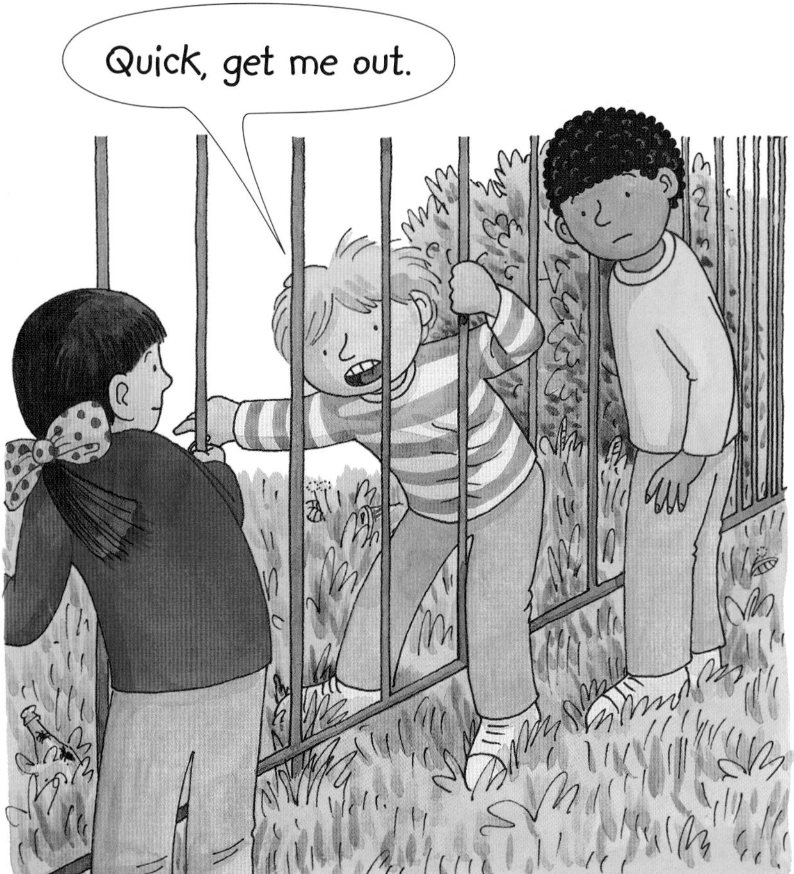
Quick, get me out.

Biff ran to get Dad.

"Kipper is stuck," said Biff.

“I can get him out,” said Dad.

"He is still stuck," said Biff.

Dad rang Mum.

"Kipper is stuck," said Dad.

Mum got a big stick.

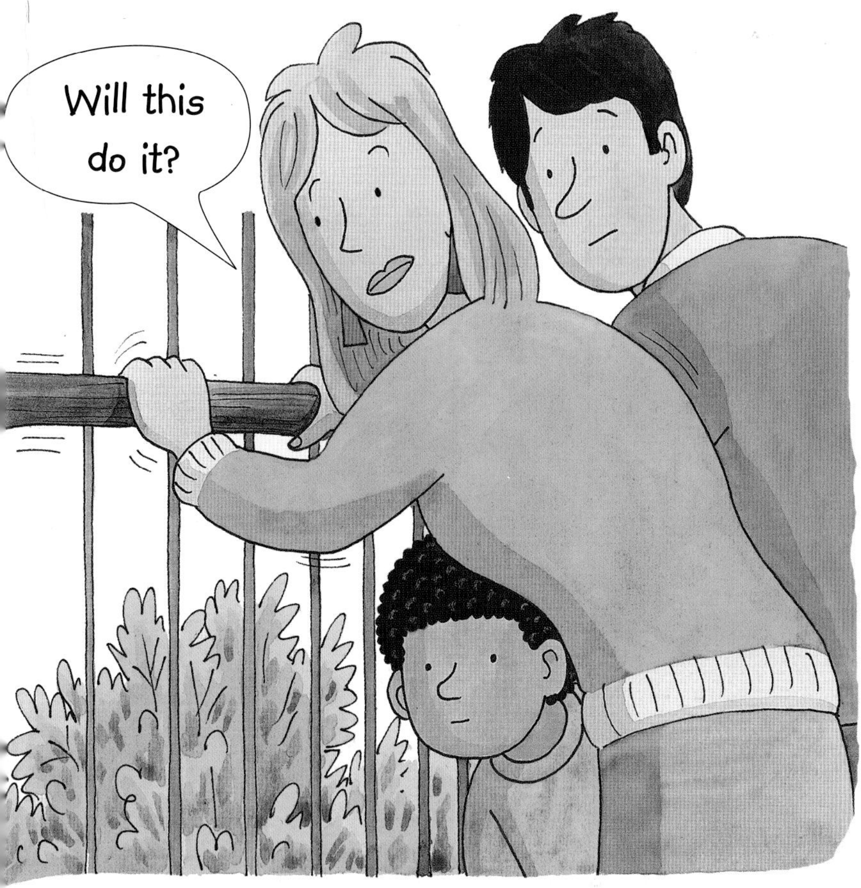
Will this do it?

"Ouch," said Kipper. "I am still stuck."

Wilma ran to get her dad.

“Kipper is stuck,” said Wilma.

Wilma's dad got his jack.

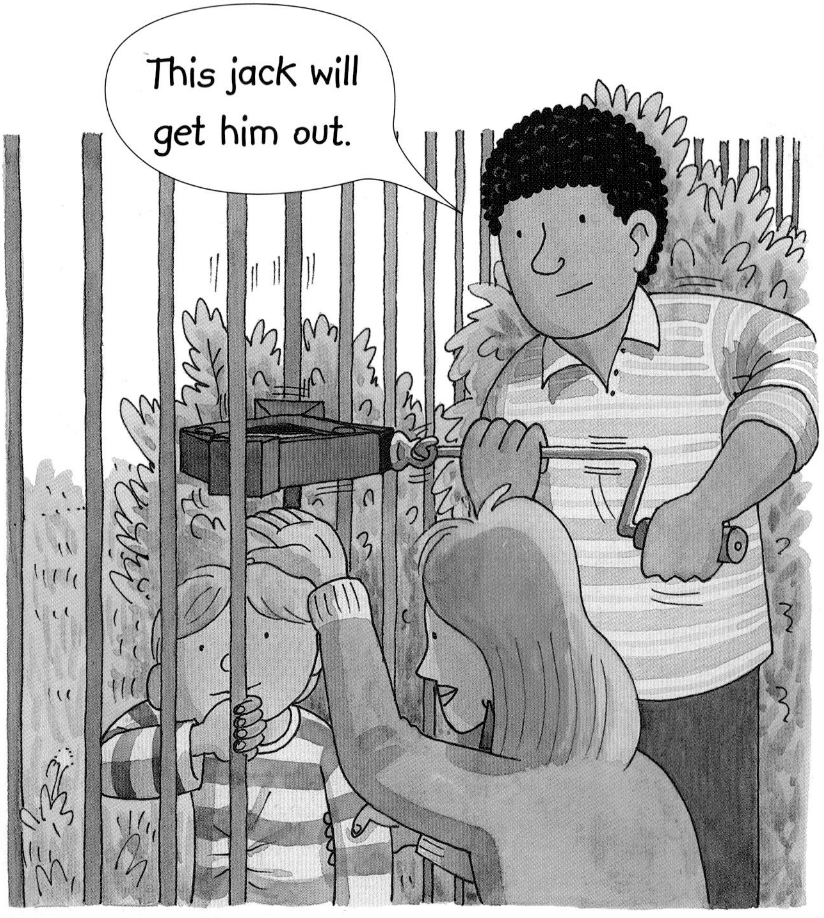
This jack will get him out.

Kipper got out.

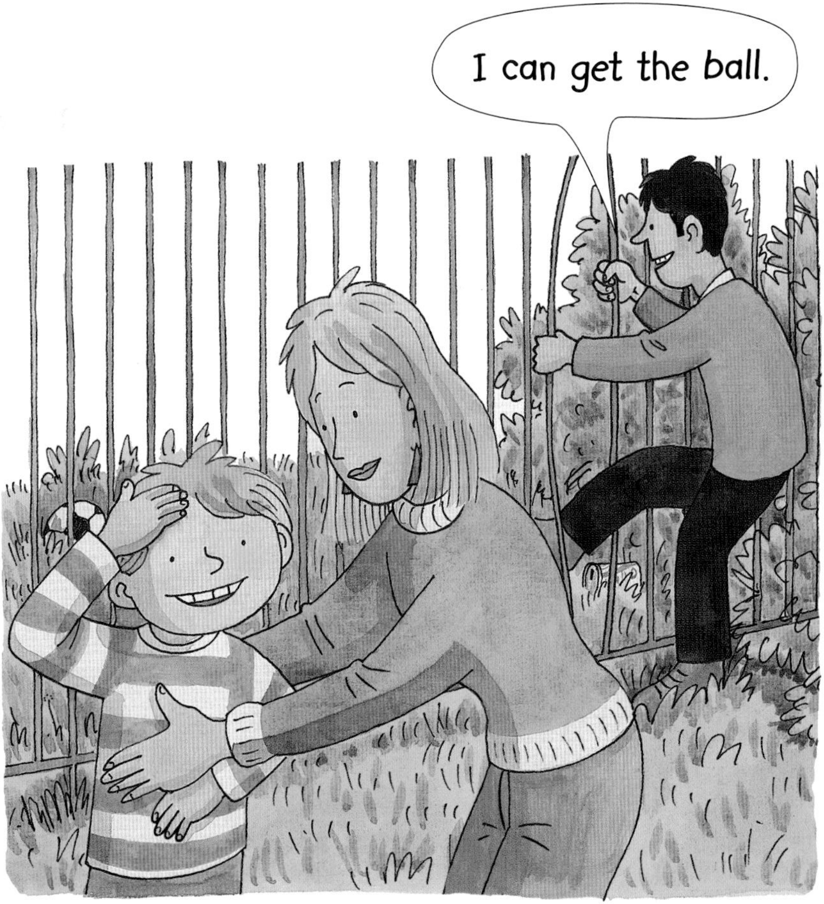
I can get the ball.

Dad was stuck.

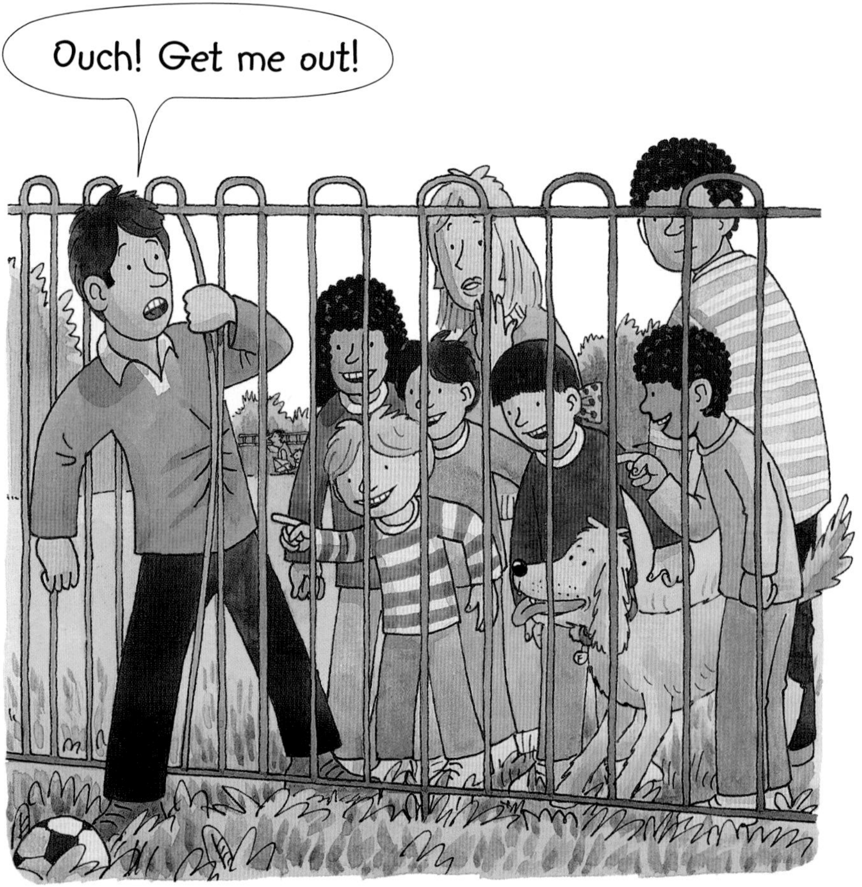
Ouch! Get me out!

Talk about the story

How did Kipper get stuck?
What did Wilma's dad use to get Kipper out?
Why did Dad get stuck?
Have you got stuck before? Where?

A maze

Help Kipper get the ball.